KU-428-809

KAZUNO KOHARA

LITTLE WIZARD

**MACMILLAN
CHILDREN'S BOOKS**

DUDLEY SCHOOLS
LIBRARY SERVICE

Schools Library and Information Services
S00000735077

DUDLEY PUBLIC LIBRARIES

L

735077   SCH

JY KOH

First published 2010 by Macmillan Children's Books
a division of Macmillan Publishers Limited
20 New Wharf Road, London N1 9RR
Basingstoke and Oxford
Associated companies throughout the world
www.panmacmillan.com

ISBN: 978-0-230-71231-7

Text and illustrations copyright © Kazuno Kohara 2010
Moral rights asserted.

All rights reserved. No part of this publication may be reproduced,
stored in or introduced into a retrieval system, or transmitted,
in any form, or by any means (electronic, mechanical, photocopying,
recording or otherwise) without the prior written permission of the
publisher. Any person who does any unauthorized act in
relation to this publication may be liable to criminal
prosecution and civil claims for damages.

1 3 5 7 9 8 6 4 2

A CIP catalogue record for this book is available
from the British Library.

Printed in Italy

Once there was a little wizard who could not learn to fly. He was always alone, because none of the other wizards wanted to be his friend.

One day, Little Wizard was walking sadly in the forest when he saw something in the sky.

It was . . .

"Hello, Dragon!" called Little Wizard. "I wish I could fly like you. Could you teach me?"

"No problem," smiled the dragon. "We can start right away."

"You must concentrate very hard," said the dragon.
"One, two, three . . ."

BUMP! It was no good. Little Wizard still could not fly.

"Don't worry!" said the dragon.
"The first flight is always the hardest.
We can practise again tomorrow."
And he invited Little Wizard to his house.

At dinnertime the dragon brought
out a basket full of bread.

"Being a dragon is very useful, when it
comes to baking bread," he said.

The next day, Little Wizard and the
dragon carried on practising.

"You need a strong will to take off," advised the dragon. "Close your eyes and think of the reason why you want to fly."

Little Wizard imagined having fun flying with the other wizards. But still nothing happened.

The dragon went home to bake some bread.
Little Wizard was still practising when he met a Knight.

"Out of my way!" said the Knight.
"I am going on a dragon hunt!"

"But the dragon in this forest is friendly,"
said Little Wizard. "And he only eats bread."

"Dragons don't eat bread!" laughed the Knight,
and he set off towards the dragon's house.

"I must warn the dragon!"
thought Little Wizard.
"But how can I get there
before the Knight?"

He climbed onto his
broomstick and held tight.
"If only I could fly!"

Little Wizard closed his eyes.
"I've got to fly, I've got to fly.
I've got to fly to save my friend!"

He felt a tingle in his feet, and
when he opened his eyes . . .

Little Wizard was **FLYING!**

In no time, he had reached the dragon's house. His friend greeted him with cheer.

"Well done, Little Wizard! Now we can go flying together!"

"Yes," replied Little Wizard.
"We must go NOW!" And he told
the dragon about the knight.

So together they flew out of the forest
and over the fields. They flew and
flew until they grew tired.

By the time they got home the knight
had given up the hunt and left the forest.
The dragon was safe.

That evening, Little Wizard and
the dragon flew up to the treetops
and ate their dinner under the stars.
The two friends talked about all the
fun they would have flying together.